JUV FIC TROUPE

Troupe, Thomas Kingsley

Robot rescue

S

ROBOT RESCUE

<Written by>: Thomas Kingsley Troupe
<Illustrated by>: Scott Burroughs

www.12StoryLibrary.com

12-Story Library is an imprint of Peterson Publishing Company
and Press Room Editions.

Produced for 12-Story Library by Red Line Editorial

Illustrations by Scott Burroughs
Technology adviser: Greg Case

ISBN
978-1-63235-231-6 (hardcover)
978-1-63235-256-9 (paperback)
978-1-62143-281-4 (hosted ebook)

Library of Congress Control Number: 2015934335

Printed in the United States of America
Mankato, MN
October, 2015

TABLE OF CONTENTS

1

HAMSTER HOUSEGUEST

Marco Martinez didn't see what all the fuss was about. Sure, hamsters were cute, and it was kind of fun to watch them run around in those little plastic balls, but it wasn't as if they were as exciting as a dog or a pet monkey.

Regardless, Dr. Whiskers, class pet of his youngest brother Felipe's third-grade class, was staying with them for the weekend.

Marco learned that every weekend some "lucky" third grader had the chance to bring the hamster home to take care of him while school was closed. After months and months of other kids being chosen, it was Felipe's turn. To say he was excited was an understatement.

"Marco!" Felipe called from the living room. "You have to see this! Dr. Whiskers just jumped out of his exercise wheel!"

Marco saved the string of code he was working on and guided his wheelchair from his bedroom into the living room, where his little brothers Rodrigo and Felipe and his dad were being entertained by the furry little guy.

All of them watched the hamster do his thing inside the little plastic "take-home" cage Dr. Whiskers lived in during weekends. The cage sat on top of the coffee table.

It has to freak that little hamster out, Marco thought, *seeing all of those giant human faces watching and reporting his every move.*

The hamster had been with them for a whole Saturday already, and by Sunday the rest of the family was still enchanted by the little rodent.

"Oh, look, now he's getting a drink of water," their dad said. "He must've worked up quite a thirst getting his exercise."

Marco rolled up to the cage and looked in. Sure enough, the light brown hamster was standing up at the inverted bottle, taking in a few delicious drops of water.

"That's pretty cool, guys," Marco said. He hoped they couldn't tell he didn't really mean it. "But I'm going back to—"

"No, wait!" Felipe shouted as if the biggest news story in the world had just broken. "He's going to work on his nest some more!"

Marco nodded and watched Dr. Whiskers tear apart a piece of paper towel they'd put in the cage earlier. The little guy shredded it in no time, adding little strips to his already built up nest of wood chips and shredded paper.

"It's like he can't decide what he wants to do!" Rodrigo exclaimed. "I can't wait to see what he does next."

Marco actually could wait, and given the choice, he would have. But, to not seem like a lame older brother, he stuck around for a few minutes, watching with the rest of his family. When he looked up at the clock, he noticed it was getting close to 6:00 p.m.

"Are we going to eat supper tonight . . . ?" Marco asked.

"Sí, Marco," his dad replied, never taking his eyes off of the cage even for a moment. "At suppertime."

"Dad, it's almost six," Marco said.

"No it's—" his dad replied, looking away to glance at the time on his cell phone. "Oh, boy. You're right."

Marco's little brothers looked at each other in shock. It was as if they couldn't believe how much time had passed since they sat down to watch the wacky adventures of Dr. Whiskers.

"Let's order some pizza," Rodrigo suggested, "so we can keep an eye on our little buddy."

"Yeah," Felipe agreed. "I have to bring him back to school tomorrow, so I don't want to miss a second."

"That's a great idea," their dad said. He looked up at Marco.

"Sure," Marco said. He didn't really care what they ate. His stomach just wanted *something.* He wondered if anyone else would've thought about supper if he hadn't mentioned it. "Pizza works for me."

"Perfect," his dad said, tossing him the cell phone. "Can you call and order it? You know what the boys and I like."

"Yeah, okay."

Marco sighed. All he wanted to do was get back to his micro-bot command module project. He was just about done, and even though he wasn't sure how, he knew Dr. Whiskers had thrown a huge monkey wrench into his progress.

As he dialed the phone number for Joey's Pizza, the living room erupted into excitement as the hamster did something else extraordinary. Marco moved his wheelchair into the kitchen to dampen the sound a bit. The girl who answered the phone asked if he could hold a moment. While waiting to place his order, he listened to the conversation among the hamster fans.

"I don't want to bring him back tomorrow," Felipe announced with a little bit of sadness in his voice.

"We should buy one of our own, Papi," Rodrigo replied. "Don't you think?"

"Dad?"

"What?" their dad asked. "Sorry, I was just watching him bury himself. It's so cute how he does that. What did you say?"

Yeah, Marco thought. *Because he's trying to hide from your goofy faces for a moment or two.*

As the Martinez brothers continued asking if they could buy a hamster of their own, Marco hoped that their dad would do the smart thing and tell them it was too much work and responsibility.

"Thanks for holding. Is this for pickup or delivery?" the girl's voice on the other end asked.

"Delivery," Marco said. After confirming his address, she asked for his order.

"We'll take a large cheese with extra cheese and a large special, hold the hamster," Marco said, still half-listening to the negotiations in the living room.

"Excuse me?"

Marco realized what he'd said and corrected himself.

"I'm sorry," he said. "I meant, hold the onions."

Yeah, Marco thought. *It'll be good to be hamster free after tonight.*

2

FURRY FREEDOM!

Monday morning was a somber one for three-fourths of the Martinez family. The talks about getting a hamster for their house didn't go well. Although their dad loved the idea of having a pet of their own, he cited one main reason that it wasn't the right time.

They had a vacation to Mexico coming in July and didn't know of anyone who would be willing to take care of their new pet. They would be gone for two weeks. Asking someone to keep the little critter fed and his cage clean would be too much.

Felipe and Rodrigo weren't happy. They had suggestions as to whom they could trust to take care of a hamster, but their dad's mind was made up.

"Not right now, boys," he said.

As their minivan pulled up in front of the school, their dad hopped out and popped the trunk. He removed Marco's wheelchair and expanded it from its compact state. Marco opened the side hatch of the vehicle as his dad rolled his wheelchair into place.

"Thanks, Dad," Marco said.

"Of course, big guy," his dad said with a smile.

They had talked about getting a mechanical lift built into their van, but Marco thought that was crazy. He could still move his arms and upper body just fine. A lift would be expensive and unnecessary, so they made do with what they had.

With his dad holding his chair still, Marco climbed in. He passed his backpack to his dad, who slung it over the back of the wheelchair handles.

"All set?" his dad asked.

"Yep," Marco replied.

"See you tonight," his dad said, giving him a hug.

"Okay, Dad," Marco replied. Most sixth graders at his school wouldn't be caught dead hugging their parents right out in the middle of the busy morning drop-off. But Marco didn't care. Since the accident, everything had changed, with Marco losing the ability to walk and his dad becoming a widower. Hugging his dad back was a no-brainer.

Once everyone else had climbed out of the van, they headed up the walkway toward Wheatley Elementary and Middle School. The school was large, with two separate buildings connected in the middle by a common area. Although it probably had seemed like a good idea to combine both schools on the same property, it made for a very crowded entryway.

"I'm going to miss Dr. Whiskers," Felipe announced, holding the small plastic cage to his chest. "The weekend went too fast."

"You'll get to see him every day," Rodrigo replied. "Like during class and stuff."

Felipe nodded, but pouted. "But not on the weekends, though."

Marco followed behind them, noticing how Felipe was slowing down the closer he got to the school. He wanted to share

any extra moment he could with the
beloved hamster.

"I'll bet Dad lets you guys get a hamster
after we come back from Mexico," Marco said.
"That's only like five months from now."

"Five months?" Felipe cried.
"That's forever!"

"What's up, Codehead?" a familiar voice
called from the crowd gathered at the front of
the school.

Marco looked up and saw fellow coding
club member Grady Hopkins standing near
the railing that lined the sidewalk. Though
the term *Codehead* might seem like an insult
to many, the members of the after-school
coding club had given themselves that name.
Somehow it seemed cooler than telling people
they were in the "coding club."

"Good morning, Grady," Marco said. They usually didn't hang out outside of the club, but lately they had gotten a little friendlier after some coding adventures.

They talked for a few minutes before the bell rang, signaling it was time for the massive crowd to come in and begin their school day. Marco followed Grady in, leaving his brothers to file in with their respective grades.

A minute or two after they were in the Commons, a central hallway between the schools, Marco heard a familiar shout and a scream.

"Whoa! What's going on?" Grady cried.

Marco glanced to his right, where the majority of the crowd was made up of kindergartners through fifth graders. People were scrambling and crying out. As he wheeled through the crowd, he found Felipe standing in the middle of the hall. The boy looked like he was about to cry.

"Felipe?" Marco asked, getting as close as he could. "Qué pasas?"

"I got bumped and I dropped the cage!" Felipe shouted.

Grady helped move people out of the way so Marco could get closer. When he was able to get his wheelchair to the edge of the crowd, he saw what had happened.

There, at his brother's feet, was the small take-home cage his family had been riveted to the night before. The top had popped off and wood shavings and papers were strewn everywhere. For a moment, Marco feared the worst. He watched as the first few tears began to stream out of his little brother's eyes.

"Dr. Whiskers," Marco said, almost like a question. "Is he . . . ?"

"He ran away," Felipe said. "I don't know where he's gone!"

Marco looked around. It felt as if there were hundreds of pairs of eyes staring at him and his little brother. Based on how crowded the hall was this morning, it didn't seem good for Dr. Whiskers.

"The hamster is named Dr. Whiskers?" Grady whispered. "Seriously? What is he a doctor of? Exercise wheels?"

Marco gave Grady a stern look and then glanced around. He half expected to hear someone scream or squish the little critter under their shoe. As much as his family's obsession with the hamster had annoyed Marco, he didn't want the poor thing to get hurt or lost.

"We have to find him, Marco," Felipe shrieked. "We just have to!"

3

SCHOOL-WIDE SEARCH

In moments, Mrs. Plotnik came over. She was Rodrigo's fourth-grade teacher who sometimes helped keep student traffic moving in the mornings. She was able to clear up the crowd and usher the gawkers to their lockers.

She let Marco stick around to console Felipe.

"It's okay," Marco urged. "We'll find him."

"What if he went outside?" Felipe said, pointing to the front doors where a few students were hurrying in.

"We don't know if he did," Marco admitted. "But we'll figure out a way to find him."

"I'll let Mr. Denny and the rest of the custodians know he's missing," Mrs. Plotnik offered. "They'll keep an eye out. I'll also see if Principal Grodichuk can make an announcement to the school. If everyone is looking for the little critter, someone will spot him."

Felipe nodded and wiped his nose with the sleeve of his shirt.

"But we need to get to class, okay?" Mrs. Plotnik said and then nodded to Marco, which he assumed was her way of saying *Thanks, I've got it from here. Please go to class.*

Marco knew that Felipe would have a hard time walking into his third-grade classroom with the empty cage. Although it was likely the entire class already knew Dr. Whiskers was on the loose, it was still going to sting.

He watched as Mrs. Plotnik walked Felipe toward the elementary school side of Wheatley. As he moved toward the hallway where the sixth-grade lockers were, he glanced around. There were a million places a tiny hamster could hide.

It wasn't until Marco's second-period social studies class that Principal Grodichuk made her special announcement.

"Attention Wheatley middle and elementary students," the principal began. "I wanted to let you all know that we have a hamster on the loose in the building. His name is . . ."

Marco listened as it sounded like Mrs. Grodichuk was fumbling with a paper to verify the hamster's name. He thought it was somewhat humorous, considering the hamster wouldn't exactly respond if called.

". . . Dr. Whiskers," she finished. "His cage was dropped in the hallway this morning. We assume he's hiding somewhere in the school. Please keep your eyes open for our little friend. If you would like to forgo recess to assist in the search, please let your teacher know. Thank you, and have a great Monday!"

The class was murmuring about the announcement when Ava Rhodes, another member of the Codeheads, tapped Marco on the shoulder.

"Are you going to help?" Ava asked.

"Yeah," Marco whispered, trying not to draw too much attention to himself. "My little brother lost him, so I kind of have to."

"I'm in, too," Ava said. "That poor little thing is probably scared stiff."

Marco nodded. He could hear some of the other students in his class joking about finding a stinky dead hamster a few months later if it didn't turn up. Although Marco wasn't really a big fan of Dr. Whiskers, it meant a lot to his brother that they find him.

As most of the school went outside for recess, Marco headed into the hallway to start the hamster search. Ava closed her locker after dropping her books inside and joined him. Marco was disappointed that no one else from the middle school seemed interested in joining the search.

"Hey, wait up," another voice called. Marco slowed and turned to see Grady running down the hall toward them.

"You're going to help us find the hamster, Hopkins?" Ava asked.

"Well, yeah," Grady said. "I used to have a hamster back in the day. I might be the best shot this thing has at surviving."

"Oh, please," Ava groaned.

"It's cool of you to help us," Marco said. "Not many of our classmates care what happens to the good doctor."

As the three members of the Codeheads crew headed into the Commons, they were surprised by how many people were gathered there. Teachers, custodial staff, and two of the cooks from the lunchroom had joined the search, too.

"Man," Grady said. "Why aren't the little kids looking for the hamster, too?"

Marco wondered the same thing at first, but then he realized why.

"They had recess an hour before our group," Marco said. "They probably already looked."

Marco noticed the searchers were spread all over. Some were walking up and down the halls, looking along the edges of the lockers. People had flashlights, looking in every crack and crevice they could find.

"They're probably scaring him away," Ava whispered.

"Right," Marco replied. "But really, how else can we expect to find him?"

In the Commons alone, there seemed to be too many places for the creature to hide. There was artwork plastered on the walls from the elementary school. The risers used in the spring program the second graders had done the week before were folded up against the wall. Bins of lost-and-found sweatshirts, jackets, and gloves lined another wall.

"Hey," Mr. Rivard, one of the gym teachers, cried. "I think I found something!"

Marco looked over to see him reaching under the risers. He and the rest of the search party in the Commons went over to see what he'd discovered.

Reaching deeper, he groaned and grabbed something. A second later, he withdrew his hand.

"False alarm," Mr. Rivard said, turning a little red. He opened his hand to show a handful of dust bunnies.

Grady came over, throwing his hands up. "I keep trying to hear the little thing but it's too loud in here."

With those words, Marco made a clicking noise with his tongue. A second later, his mind lit up.

"That just gave me a great idea," Marco said, reaching into his backpack. He fished around until he found what he was looking for.

Ava sighed. "Oh," she said. "That thing again?"

4

ELECTRONIC EARS

Marco held the little device he'd built a few months ago. It was a small box-shaped module with a number of gadgets attached to it. It was able to detect changes in temperature, record audio, and capture video.

"Yes!" Marco said. "We can place this somewhere a hamster might hide. If it picks up any noise, it'll record the sound and send me a text message on my phone."

"Okay," Ava said. "But where are you going to put that? We have no idea at all where to start."

"Yeah, that's tough, man," Grady said. "That hamster could be a long way from here. We don't even know if he's in the Commons or somewhere else. That little guy could be hiding in tons of places."

Marco shrugged. "We have to start somewhere."

He pulled his laptop out of his backpack and opened it up.

"You going to do some coding right here on the spot?" Grady asked. "We don't have that much time."

"Just a quick change to the device's settings," Marco said, opening up the program he'd developed for the device. "I modified this thing a bit so that I could easily add and remove the triggers. I'll just swap out the temperature plugin for the audio plugin. It was set to trigger when the temperature changed, initially. Now I want it to listen for any strange noises, but within a limited range."

"Why not have it listen to everything?" Ava asked.

Marco punched in a few commands and compiled his code.

"Well, you know how noisy this place is. If it sent me a message anytime it heard anything, I'd be getting thousands of text messages," Marco explained.

"Makes sense," Ava said, nodding.

"Okay," Marco said. "Where do we put it?"

"Yeah, hamster expert," Ava said. "What do you think?"

Grady looked around, as if trying to assess the best spot.

"Well, hamsters like to hide in enclosed spaces," Grady began. "Maybe by those lockers over there?"

Marco looked. On the elementary side of the school there was a bank of blue lockers. Along the edge of the lockers, he saw a small dark gap. If he were a hamster looking to hide out, the spot would be just about perfect.

"Let's do it," Marco said, glancing up at the clock. They didn't have a ton of time, but he thought it was worth a shot. The three of them positioned the device near the gap in the lockers.

"I just hope we didn't scare it even more," Ava said, backing away from their position as if Marco had just planted a bomb.

Marco and Grady followed her into the Commons and waited.

"If it detects anything, it'll send me a text with an audio clip in the message," Marco said. "We can listen to it and see if there's any sort of hamster-like sounds."

They continued to search the vicinity of the Commons and hallways. Just as the recess bell was about to ring, Marco's cell phone vibrated.

Message received.

"Guys," Marco called. "I've got one!"

Ava and Grady joined him as he opened the text. Just as he'd programmed, there was an embedded link to an audio file in the message. He touched the blue hyperlink, and the audio file opened.

What followed was a short three-second rustling sound.

"That's it?" Ava asked, as if disappointed by their audio capture.

"It sounds like something moving around!" Grady gasped, clearly more excited. "Like a hamster rustling around or whatever."

Marco nodded. "Let's check it out!"

The three of them raced back to where the device had been placed, and Grady got down on his knees to peer into the hole.

"Can you see anything?" Marco asked.

"No," Grady said. "But I might be able to reach my fingers in there."

"Don't get them bitten off," Ava teased.

"Oh, whatever," Grady said, shaking his head. He poked his pointer finger inside.

"Anything?" Marco asked.

"Yeah," Grady said and pulled his finger out. He dragged a small piece of paper that looked like a gum wrapper with him.

"Ugh," Ava said. "That doesn't help."

Marco looked at the wrapper as Grady stood up and dusted off the knees of his jeans.

"Maybe someone walking by made the wrapper inside the hole move a bit," Marco suggested, "enough to trigger the device."

"Well, this sort of tells me something," Grady said. "The hamster probably didn't come through here. If Dr. Whiskers came across this sweet piece of paper, he'd probably take it and shred it."

"Not if he was too scared to stop," Ava argued. "If I had a school full of humans looking for me, you think I'd stop to shred stuff up?"

"Maybe," Grady said. "It probably depends on how safe you thought you were."

No one said anything. Marco glanced over at the rest of the search party. People seemed to have stopped looking for the hamster and were talking among themselves.

They probably feel like we do, Marco thought. *Like this is an impossible mission.*

"What if we could set a trap or something for him?" Ava asked.

"We don't want to kill the thing!" Grady cried, obviously alarmed.

"No, no," Ava said. "Like a humane trap. They sell those at stores, I think. We could fill it with hamster food and one of those things they like to run around in."

"An exercise wheel," Grady said.

"Yeah," Ava said. "Put out some nice colorful paper for it to chew on. Really draw the hamster in. How could he resist?"

Once Ava said that, Marco glanced over at the wall in the Commons. Art projects hung along the wall. They were taped as high as any of the teachers could reach and as low as the carpeted floor.

One of the projects stuck out to Marco.

"Guys," he said, turning his wheelchair toward the Commons. "Grab the device. I think I see something."

Grady snapped up the little box.

"What about the trap?" Ava asked.

"I don't think we'll need it," Marco replied.

5

ART ATTACK

"Look at this," Marco said as he wheeled closer to the art projects.

It appeared that Ms. Diaz's third-grade class was especially proud of the artwork in which the students had reproduced their own homes with construction paper. There were cutout brown paper roofs, multicolored houses, yellow suns, and strips of green grass along the bottoms of their masterpieces.

"Nice," Grady said. "Those are some pretty sweet houses, Marco. But is this really the time to appreciate third-grade artistry?"

Marco laughed but pointed.

"No," he said. "Look closer."

At the bottom of a paper with the name "Paige W." scribbled at the top, a section of construction paper grass looked torn away.

"Whoa," Grady said. "Looks like Dr. Whiskers is collecting paper after all."

"How do we know that it wasn't just torn?" Ava asked.

Grady squatted down and Ava followed his lead. Marco turned sideways for a closer look, too.

"Look," Grady said. "You can see little bite marks along the bottom of the paper."

"So does Dr. Whiskers eat paper?" Ava asked.

"No, no," Grady said. "Hamsters do that to build nests. He's probably looking for a place to call home since he lost his old one."

Marco thought about this. On the one hand it meant that Dr. Whiskers was still alive. But it still didn't help them narrow down his location. Using the device was a good idea, but he knew that the Commons was typically a busy place and would continue to give them false audio leads.

As the bell rang, signaling the end of recess, Marco's mind began to work.

"I might have an idea," he said as they turned to head back to their lockers.

"Good," Grady said. "Because while Dr. Whiskers might be building a nest somewhere, he's probably going to get hungry."

There was no news about anyone locating Dr. Whiskers for the rest of the morning. Marco decided to spend his lunch in the computer room.

He wasn't surprised to see the Codeheads adviser, Mrs. Donovan, in there, eating her lunch while staring at the computer.

"Working lunch, Marco?" she asked through a mouthful of pasta salad.

"Yes," Marco replied. "I've got something I think might help find the missing hamster."

"Good," Mrs. Donovan said, swallowing her bite. "I hope you find that little guy. I'm not a fan of rodents."

Marco smiled. He'd stopped thinking of the hamster as a rodent sometime during the morning. He realized he had really begun to care about the furry little guy and wanted him to be safe. *Rodent* seemed like a dirty word to him now, a word to describe rats or shrews.

He opened up a web browser and did a search for hamster sounds. Although Dr. Whiskers wasn't really a noisy little fellow, Marco had heard him squeak and chitter.

Some quick research showed Marco that he was onto something.

"When a hamster squeaks, it usually means he is agitated or afraid of something," Marco whispered to himself. "This happens when a hamster is introduced to a new environment but will stop when he becomes used to it, usually after a few days."

If Dr. Whiskers is able to find a place to settle down, he's going to stop making noise, Marco thought. *Time really is of the essence!*

Marco ran another search, this time looking for audio files of hamster noises. In no time he located a number of examples. He downloaded them and moved them into a folder. He pulled up the program for his device and changed the parameters. Using an open source audio analysis program, he analyzed the samples and generated an audio fingerprint. Just like a real fingerprint, it would match only if the sound had the same characteristics as a real hamster squeak. Marco instructed the program to text him with an audio file only if it heard something "hamster-like."

Moving quickly, Marco compiled the code and checked for any errors. Closing up his workstation, Marco turned and headed for the door.

"Just like that?" Mrs. Donovan asked.

"We'll see," Marco said. "See you after school!"

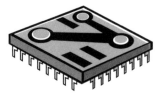

Marco headed back to the Commons with his newly configured device. Though he couldn't sit around and wait for the hamster to make noise, he wanted to position it and at least see what sorts of sounds he could capture.

"Hey, Marco," Grady called, approaching from the hallway. "Did you find him?"

"No," Marco said, "but I've configured the device to only send me audio samples that sound like a hamster."

"Sweet," Grady said. "So it'll ignore all the other sounds?"

"In theory," Marco said. "Didn't have a chance to test it out."

Marco and Grady positioned the hamster monitoring device (or HMD, as Grady called it), trying their best to keep it out of view. Marco didn't want some curious student to pick it up and walk off with it.

They set the device just underneath the torn art project and closer to the Commons' large trophy case.

"Now what?" Grady asked, standing up.

The bell rang, signaling the end of lunch and the beginning of fifth period.

"Now we wait," Marco said and held up his phone.

6

CRITTER CHATTER

It was about twenty minutes into Marco's English class when his cell phone vibrated. He knew the rule about using phones in class, so he let it sit. It took every ounce of his willpower.

He imagined the little sounds of Dr. Whiskers, calling for help somewhere in the Commons area.

Maybe he's hurt or lonely, Marco thought, almost reaching into his jeans pocket. *No, I can't. I have to wait. I don't want Mr. Vang to take my phone away. Then I'd be really sunk!*

Mr. Vang read something from their textbook and asked the rest of the class to follow along. As Marco turned the page, his phone vibrated again.

Another message.

And again.

Three! Marco thought. *This thing is working like a charm. That little guy must be making all kinds of noise!*

By the time the class was over, Marco had seven messages. Once they were dismissed, Marco rolled as fast as he could into the hallway.

Ava and Grady were waiting by his locker.

"I told Ava what you were up to," Grady said. "Did you get anything?"

"Seven," Marco said, unlocking his phone and accessing the messaging app.

"Seven? That's crazy," Grady said. "Dr. W must be going nuts!"

Though time was precious before the start of sixth period, the Codeheads played the messages, one by one. They huddled around Marco's wheelchair, pressing their ears as close to the phone as they could.

The first message was the sound of a squeaking chair. The second was another squeak.

"Sounds like a squeaky tennis shoe," Ava reasoned.

"These squeaks must have triggered the fingerprint because it's in the same frequency range as a hamster squeak," Marco explained.

"I have no idea what you just said," Grady muttered. "Hit the next one."

Each consecutive message after that was some sort of high-pitched sound that could be easily explained away. These sounds weren't made by a hamster. Seeing that the bell was about to ring, Marco quickly tried the sixth message.

The glorious sounds of a hamster squeaking chittered through his phone's speakers.

"Is that . . . ?" Ava asked, her eyes wide with excitement.

"Yeah, man," Grady replied. "That's hamster for: *Help me, Codeheads. You're my only hope.*"

"We found him," Marco whispered. He played the last message and was happy to hear there were more hamster sounds. "Or at least we're close. He has to be somewhere near the device. It has a limited range, but Dr. Whiskers didn't sound too far away."

The bell rang, signaling the start of sixth period.

"I have a test, otherwise I'd see if I could look around," Ava mumbled.

"Me too," Marco said. "I'm guessing we can hold out until coding club after school."

"Sure," Grady said. "If the little dude is building a nest, he's probably not going anywhere."

The last two classes of the day dragged. During that time, Marco ended up with seventeen more messages. He listened to them in between classes and played the last two on his way to the Commons.

Grady and Ava were already there.

"I'll bet he's behind this trophy case," Grady said.

"Can you see anything?" Marco asked, slipping his phone into his pocket.

Grady pressed his face against the wall and closed one eye as if that would help him see a little better. He looked like a deranged pirate squinting into the wrong end of a spy glass.

"You're going to scare him off with a face like that," Ava joked.

"Very funny," Grady said. "But I can't see a thing. It's dark and there are all kinds of little dust bunnies and stuff."

Marco looked at the trophy case. There was a small gap between the giant wooden case and the wall, big enough for a little hamster to seek refuge from the morning crowd in the Commons. The case was filled with trophies from the middle school basketball, volleyball, and football teams.

"Can we move it?" Ava asked.

"I doubt it," Marco said. "Besides, we don't know for sure Dr. W is back there. We're just assuming he is because the HMD picked up his squeaks."

"We could find Marv Denny, the school custodian," Grady suggested. "He and some of the other guys could probably move it."

Marco shrugged. "We need to be sure," he said. "Grab the HMD. I've got an idea."

The Codeheads joined the rest of their group in the computer room. Mrs. Donovan was standing at the dry-erase board explaining a new piece of configuration code.

"You guys still looking for that little rat?" Miles Patrick asked. He sat next to

Travis Jacobson and smirked as if he'd said something funny. Tara Calhoun looked up from her cell phone.

"If you find it, don't bring it in here," Tara warned. "Right, Mrs. Donovan?"

Marco wheeled over to an open workstation and opened his laptop. He turned in his seat and reached into his backpack. He produced a small contraption that looked like a tiny robot with tank treads instead of legs.

"Oh, wow," Grady said. "You've been waiting to use him."

Marco smiled. As his mind began to work, he made small clicking sounds with his tongue. He took the HMD and held it up to his micro-bot, which he'd named Mike.

Marco pulled up a coding window. He accessed his control module for Mike and opened the code he used for the HMD.

Copying several lines of code, he switched
to the other window and dropped it into the
micro-bot page.

"What are you doing?" Ava asked.

"I'm going to rig the HMD to Mike," Marco
said. "I just need to pull the code I need for
the device's video camera."

"So you're going to send Mike behind the trophy case?" Grady asked. "Like a recon mission?"

"Yes," Marco said, without looking up from his work.

Grady clapped Marco on the back in excitement.

"Oh, man!" Grady cried. "This is so cool!"

"It will be if I can get the camera to shoot over his head," Marco whispered. "See if you can find some sort of strong tape."

As Grady looked for the tape, Marco deleted some of the parameters from the source code.

Hang on, Dr. Whiskers, Marco thought. *We're coming!*

7

MOVIE MIKE

Though Marco never intended for it to happen, he had the entire Codeheads crew hovering over his shoulders, including Mrs. Donovan.

Grady had found some electrical tape in Mrs. Donovan's desk, after being reminded he needed to ask before he rooted around for supplies in another person's workspace. Very carefully, Marco strapped the HMD to the back of the small, treaded micro-bot.

"It's like he's got a high-tech backpack on or something," Travis said.

Marco nodded. He'd designed the devices to work independently of each other and hadn't thought to combine them before. He managed to get the little light for the camera to work. It was pretty dark behind the trophy case.

"Now," Marco said, double clicking an app on his laptop, "let's see if we get any sort of picture from this."

A window opened and a small circle spun in the middle of the dark screen, showing that the program was loading. After a moment, the workstation next to Marco's was displayed. A second later, Grady's giant face appeared on the screen.

"Hey," Grady said, tilting his head. "Can you guys see up my nose?"

"Yeah," Ava said. "And it's terrifying."

Perfect, Marco thought. *We'll have a live feed!*

"Did you ever figure out how to get him to move the way you want?" Ava asked.

Marco took a deep breath. He'd been working on Mike for a good chunk of the school year already. His first attempt had been to have him walk on legs. The problem was, Mike's upper body and head were too bulky, making him top-heavy and prone to tip over.

Marco had installed the treads a month or two back and was able to get the robot to move, but not always as smoothly as he'd like.

"Mostly," Marco admitted after a moment. "He's still a little buggy."

Marco didn't think it would be too hard to get Mike to squeeze into the gap with his new accessory pack. There wasn't much room for him to move, so it wasn't like Mike would need to make left or right turns once he was behind the trophy case.

The group watched Marco do a few test runs with the micro-bot along the desk. He was slow moving, burdened a bit by the HMD strapped to his back. Marco was just relieved that he didn't tip over.

"Okay," Marco said, amazed that everyone was still watching him. "Let's send in Mike."

As the group moved into the Commons, they were surprised to see other people there, still looking for the hamster. Marco's younger brothers, Felipe and Rodrigo, were there.

"We still can't find him, Marco!" Felipe cried. His eyes looked red, as though he'd been crying recently. "I'm worried he's—"

"Don't even think that way, hermano," Marco said. "We might've found him."

"We've looked everywhere!" Rodrigo said, joining them. "The teachers are beginning to think he's long gone."

"We'll see," Marco said as he moved to the trophy case. He handed the little robot to Grady, who squatted down between the ravaged third-grade art and the trophy case. He set Mike down on the carpeted floor, moving him closer to the gap between the wall and the wood.

"We looked behind there," Felipe said, standing next to his older brother's wheelchair. "Ms. Diaz even shone a flashlight around."

Marco nodded. On his laptop, he opened up his interface and typed the first command for Mike, directing him to move forward.

The little robot hitched for a second, and Marco was afraid his program was going to crash. But after a moment, the robot moved forward.

"Let's see what we see," Marco said.

8

SWEET SURPRISE

Marco opened up the video feed window and positioned it next to his command window. The crowd mumbled behind him, amazed at how well they could see.

"I really should get the custodians," Grady said. "Wonder if they have any idea how filthy it is back there."

It was true. There were large, gray, wispy dust bunnies that threatened to block the tiny camera lens. But Mike was a trooper, forging ahead through the dust and debris behind the giant trophy case.

"I don't see anything," Ava whispered from Marco's right. "Maybe he moved—"

It was then that they could hear the small, squeaky chirps. Marco's heart raced a bit with excitement. He quickly commanded Mike to stop moving forward.

Dr. Whiskers was close!

"Okay," Marco said, trying to keep his voice down. Though he was too far away to scare the hamster, it felt as if he were right behind the case, seeing what his little robot was seeing. "Let's see if we can turn a bit."

Marco punched in the command, making the robot turn slightly to the left. It was a tight squeeze, but Mike managed, aiming his camera at a different angle. As he did, something moved quickly past the camera and out of the frame.

"Did you see that?" Miles called from behind Marco.

"It looked like a stubby little tail," Grady whispered quickly.

"Gross," Tara said.

Marco studied the screen. From what he could tell, there was a little gap underneath the base of the trophy case. If Dr. Whiskers was truly back there, it would make sense that he'd hide under the gap. The problem was, Mike would never fit under there.

"Turn just a little more," Marco whispered. He typed in another command, getting Mike to pivot slightly. The camera jolted a bit and Mike tipped over.

"No!" Grady shouted.

"Wait," Marco said, watching the autofocus on the mini-camera adjust itself. When it did, he discovered that the "fall" Mike had taken was a stroke of dumb luck. "It's aiming at the gap beneath the case!"

When the screen was brought into focus, Marco and the rest of the onlookers gasped. There, in the darkness under the Wheatley Middle School trophy case, were a pair of shiny eyes peering at them.

"Dr. Whiskers!" Felipe shouted. "You found him!"

"I'll call the custodians," Mrs. Donovan said from the back of the crowd.

Marco smiled as he watched the monitor. Dr. Whiskers had been busy building himself a little nest. There were colored strips of paper huddled together in the dark, borrowed from the third-grade art projects that hung nearby.

A second later, a tiny pink face could be seen, then another, and then another.

"How many hamsters are under there?" Marco wondered aloud.

"Those look like—" Ava began.

"Babies!" Marco finished.

Grady slapped his forehead with his hand. "Of course!" he cried. "That's why he made a nest. He—"

"*She*," Ava corrected.

"She was getting ready to have her litter of little hamsters!" Grady exclaimed.

"So Dr. Whiskers is a girl hamster?" Felipe asked.

"Dr. Whiskers is a mom," Marco said.

It took almost twenty minutes for the custodians and the students to carefully remove the trophies and move the case away from the wall. Dr. Whiskers stayed with her babies the whole time, crouched low in her colorful nest.

The crowd gathered around and Marco counted nine babies in Dr. Whiskers's litter. They were pink little things that squirmed around their mom, hungry and cold.

"Hmmm," Ms. Diaz, Felipe's third-grade teacher, murmured. "We have more than enough hamsters for every third-grade class to have one."

After Ms. Diaz had slipped a file folder under the nest and hamsters, she gently placed them in Dr. Whiskers's cage. Grady retrieved Mike and dusted him off before handing him to Marco.

"His first mission was a success," Grady said, folding his arms across his chest.

"It was," Marco said, watching his younger brother follow Ms. Diaz down the hall.

"Little Mike was a micro-bot hero," Ava said, nodding toward the tiny robot.

"Yeah, but I'll need to figure out how to get him to stay upright," Marco said, unstrapping the HMD from his micro-bot. "I'm betting I can add some weight to his treads or—"

"Marco," Ava said. "Just enjoy the victory, man. You totally saved a hamster and her little babies. You and Mike are heroes."

Marco nodded and shrugged. It *did* feel pretty good.

A moment later, Felipe came running back with Ms. Diaz close behind.

"Marco!" Felipe shouted. "Ms. Diaz said we can take one of the hamsters home!"

"But we'll be in Mexico for a few weeks this summer," Marco said. He looked at Ms. Diaz. "My dad said—"

"We'll talk with your dad," Ms. Diaz said. "But maybe I can watch over the little one until your family returns."

"Yeah, maybe that'll work," Marco said with a smile.

He knew his dad wouldn't be able to
resist having a little hamster of their own. And
truth be told, neither could Marco.

THE END

1. When Marco's family is watching Dr. Whiskers, Marco gets a little irritated. Why do you think he feels this way? Use evidence from the story to support your answer.

2. Dr. Whiskers is lost, and Marco feels he should help look for her. Why would he want to do something like that? Use examples from the book as proof.

3. The Codeheads used many clues to find Dr. Whiskers. What were they? How did they help?

WRITE ABOUT IT

1. In this book, Felipe was responsible for something really important in watching the class hamster. Write a story about a time when you were put in charge of something. What was it? Did you do a good job? Be sure to include these details in your story.

2. Grady used his expertise as a former hamster owner to help Marco find Dr. Whiskers. Write a story about something you know well. What is it? Do you share this information with others? Is it helpful?

3. Write a story from the perspective of Dr. Whiskers after she gets lost. What is it like to be lost in the school?

ABOUT THE AUTHOR

Thomas Kingsley Troupe started writing stories when he was in second grade. Since then, he's authored more than sixty fiction and nonfiction books for kids. Born and raised in "Nordeast" Minneapolis, he now lives in Woodbury, Minnesota. In his spare time, he enjoys spending time with his family, conducting paranormal investigations, and watching movies with the Friends of Cinema. One of his favorite words is *delicious*.

ABOUT THE ILLUSTRATOR

Scott Burroughs graduated from the San Francisco, California, Academy of Art University in 1994 with a BFA in illustration. Upon graduating, he was hired by Sega of America as a conceptual artist and animator. In 1995, he completed the Walt Disney Feature Animation Internship program and was hired as an animator. While at Disney, he was an animator, a mentor for new artists, and a member of the Portfolio Review Board. He worked at the Disney Florida Studio until it closed its doors in 2005. Since 2005, Scott has been illustrating everything from children's books to advertisements and editorials, just to name a few. Scott is also a published author of several children's books. He resides in northern California with his high school sweetheart/wife and two sons.

MORE FUN WITH THE CODING CLUB

GAMER BANDIT

When a mysterious lunch thief leaves behind a card with a website address, Ava Rhodes can't help but check it out. After the site leads her to a really boring online video game, she's even more determined. Can GPS tracking help Ava and her friends find the thief? Or will more lunches go missing?

HACK ATTACK

After a hacker breaches the school's grading system and gives students failing grades, Grady Hopkins wants to set the record straight. Along with coders Ava and Marco, Grady follows a trail of IP addresses as he searches for the perpetrator. Will they find the truth before everyone flunks sixth grade?

NABBED TABLET

When Ava Rhodes's brand new tablet computer goes missing, she's desperate to solve the mystery. Can her fellow coding club members Marco and Grady and some quick coding help her? Or is everyone a suspect?

READ MORE FROM 12-STORY LIBRARY

Every 12-Story Library book is available in many formats, including Amazon Kindle and Apple iBooks. For more information, visit your device's store or 12StoryLibrary.com.